Be Well, Beware

"Should I walk her?" Lily asks. That is what she's always heard you are supposed to do for a horse

"]

Shor

rolli

her

with

pass

Gra

bett

wor:

Jessie Haas

Be Well, Beware

Pictures by Jos. A. Smith

A Beech Tree Paperback Book
New York

Text copyright © 1996 by Jessie Haas
Illustrations copyright © 1996 by Jos. A. Smith

The Library of Congress has cataloged the Greenwillow Books edition of *Be
Well, Beware* as follows:

Haas, Jessie.
Be well, Beware / by Jessie Haas ;
pictures by Jos. A. Smith.
     p. cm.
Summary: Lily is frightened when her beloved horse Beware gets sick and
exhibits peculiar behavior.
ISBN 0-688-14545-0
[1. Horses—Fiction.]
I. Smith, Jos. A. (Joseph Anthony) (date), ill.
II. Title.
PZ7.H1129Bd 1996 [Fic]—dc20 95-16718 CIP AC

10 9 8 7 6 5 4 3 2 1
First Beech Tree Edition, 1997
ISBN 0-688-15420-4

To Josey, again,
and to Dr. Ron Svec, who saved her life

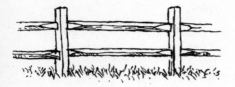

CHAPTER ONE

THE SCHOOL BUS sounds as if it's dying by the time it winds up through the hills to Lily's stop. There are hardly any kids left.

Lily waves good-bye to Mandy and jumps down the steps. She runs up the long driveway, swinging her backpack, kicking the crisp, dry leaves. The leaves are like a bowlful of cornflakes before you put the milk in.

At the top of the drive Lily looks toward the horse pasture. She sees the pony grazing. Beware must be nearby. Lily hurries into the house. It gets dark very early now that fall is here. There is just barely time for a ride.

The kitchen smells like apple crisp. Gran turns from the stove. "Hello, Lily. Did you have a good—" But Lily is already past her, running up the stairs.

Quickly, quickly. She pulls off her jeans and her good sweater, pulls on her riding pants and a sweatshirt. Pushes her feet into her riding boots. Down the stairs again.

"It's more polite to say hello!" says Gran.

"Oh, hello, Gran." There is a plate of apple cores on the table. "Can I have these for Beware?"

Gran snorts. "*May* I, please! Yes, you may. Heaven forbid we should deny anything to a horse . . ." Lily lets the door bang behind her.

"Sorry, Gran," she calls.

The sun has gone down behind the mountain. The air feels cold on Lily's hands. Two sweatshirts would be better than one, but Lily doesn't have time to go back upstairs. She gets a halter and walks down to the gate. "Beware!"

The pony lifts his head and looks at Lily.

"Beware!" Lily looks toward the trees along the edge of the pasture. In the summer Beware stands there in the shade. Now the trees are bare, and it's too cold to care about shade.

"Hey, Beware!" Lily yells. Has something happened? Lily puts the apple cores on the ground beside the gate and ducks under the fence. Then she reaches back and grabs one. "Beware?"

From the tree line Beware whinnies.

Now Lily can see her. Beware's dark red coat blends in with the tree trunks, until you know where to look. Lily stands still and whistles. "Apple core! Come and get it!"

Beware whinnies again. But she doesn't move.

All at once Lily knows. Something is wrong. Beware is caught in wire, or she's hurt herself. Otherwise she'd come down the hill. She wouldn't just stand there. . . . Lily is running. The buckle of the halter whips against her legs. The cold air burns in her chest.

Beware turns her head. She whinnies loudly. But she doesn't move. All four legs stay in exactly the same place, as still as the tree trunks. She must be caught in wire.

But when Lily reaches Beware, she can't see any wire anywhere. Only dead leaves and sticks and Beware's four feet, standing still.

Beware reaches her nose out to Lily. She brushes her upper lip across the apple core and knocks it into the leaves. She stretches for it. But the apple core has rolled past where Beware can reach. She won't go after it, not even one tiny step.

"Oh, Beware!" Lily buckles the halter onto Beware's head. Her fingers are shaking. "Okay now, walk."

Beware doesn't move.

Lily pulls on the halter. "Beware, *walk!*" She makes her voice loud and stern. If Beware takes even a few steps, maybe Lily can tell what's wrong.

Lily pulls hard on the halter. Beware's neck stretches out straight. When her neck won't stretch any longer, Beware takes a step. And another. Her front feet seem normal, but her back feet stumble and waver. Her back legs aren't working right. When Lily stops pulling, Beware stops walking. But she reaches down and finds the apple core and crunches it slowly.

Lily goes behind Beware and looks at her back legs. There are no cuts and no bumps. When she runs her hands down Beware's legs, Beware does not flinch. But when Lily pushes on Beware's rump and tells her to walk, Beware's back legs buckle, and she almost falls down.

For a moment Lily just stands there, hugging her sides. What can be the matter? Beware isn't rolling or kicking at her stomach, so it can't be colic. She doesn't seem to have a broken leg. But she can't move. Has she hurt her spine? Has she been poisoned?

Gramp would know. But Gramp isn't home yet, and Mom isn't home yet, and Gran doesn't like horses.

There's only one thing to do. "I'll be right back!" And Lily is flying down the hill. There is no time to wait, no time to guess what might be wrong. Lily has to get a vet here. Right away.

CHAPTER TWO

Gʀᴀɴ ʟᴏᴏᴋs ᴜᴘ when Lily bursts through the door. "Lily! What—"

"Beware's sick!" Lily turns the pages of the phone book. She can't remember the vet's name. She can't even remember the alphabet.

"Here." Gran points to a phone number taped on the wall. Lily dials.

"Valley Vet Clinic," a woman's voice says.

"Is one of the vets there?"

"Dr. Shore is out on a call," the woman says, "but I can reach him. Is this an emergency?"

"Yes!"

"What's the nature of the problem?"

Suddenly Lily can hardly speak. "My horse—she can't move. She's way out in the pasture, and she can't move her back legs—"

"Is she standing?" The woman's voice sounds sharper. She sounds worried, too.

"Yes," Lily says.

"I'll get through to Dr. Shore and have him call you. Who is this?"

"Lily Griffin."

"Woody's granddaughter?" Now the woman sounds even more concerned. "Dr. Shore's at a farm not too far from you. I'll have him call right away. Don't you worry, honey." The woman hangs up without saying good-bye.

Gran is peeling potatoes. Peel after peel flops into the scrap bucket. She doesn't need to look at the potatoes. She looks at Lily.

"Will she eat?"

"She ate an apple core." Lily's eyes want to cry, but she feels too cold inside, too scared. "Dr. Shore's going to call."

"I'll talk to him. You go back to her. Take a hand-ful of hay, Lily, and some water—not a big bucket!" Gran warns as Lily goes out the door. "Don't you hurt your back!"

It's so cold. Lily shivers inside her sweatshirt. It takes a long time to climb back up the hill with the heavy pail of water. Beware looks tiny and far away.

The pony comes to see what's in the pail. He doesn't want water, but he steals a snatch of hay. He follows behind Lily, crunching, and he steals another mouthful.

Beware whinnies when Lily gets close. Her voice sounds loud and worried. She sniffs the water and takes a sip. Slowly she winds a wisp of hay into her mouth and chews.

If only Beware could speak! If only she could say what's wrong!

Lily looks again for bumps or cuts. She runs her hands down Beware's legs. If Beware had a broken leg, it would hurt when Lily touched it. But Beware doesn't flinch.

Lily presses her fingers along Beware's spine. She

presses softly at first and then harder. That doesn't seem to hurt either.

She feels the tips of Beware's ears. Sometimes if a horse has a fever, its ears will feel hot. Or if it is very sick, or dying, its ears will feel cold.

Beware's ears feel normal, and she is eating slowly. Very sick horses usually don't eat at all.

But there *is* something wrong! It doesn't make sense!

Lily leans on Beware's warm shoulder. She smells Beware's rich horse smell. She reaches under Beware's belly to scratch. Beware loves to have her tummy scratched.

As Lily's hand slides down Beware's side, she notices something. She steps back to look.

A ridge of muscle shows along Beware's round side. Usually Lily can't see that muscle. Now it's hard and tight. Lily goes to Beware's other side. The muscle shows there, too. What could that mean?

"Lily?"

A small figure is coming across the field. Gramp? The vet?

No, it is only Gran, wearing Gramp's old coat over her dress and a pair of big black boots. She comes steadily up the hill.

"Dr. Shore is on his way," Gran says. "He'll be here in twenty minutes." She waits a moment to get her breath. "Be about dark by then—don't know how he can work on her when he can't see."

Lily has thought of that. "Could we drive the tractor up and shine the headlights on her?"

"That's an idea," says Gran. "Better to get her down, though. Will walking do her any harm, do you think?"

"I don't know," Lily says. "I don't think she has anything broken."

"Let's try," Gran says. She goes behind Beware, pushing the pony aside. "Out of my way, you foolish thing!" Gran puts her shoulder against Beware's rump. Her cheek is close to Beware's hip, and her glasses gleam as she nods to Lily. "Now pull," she says.

Lily pulls on the halter rope. Gran pushes with her shoulder. Beware takes a wobbly step.

"Again!" says Gran. They push, and pull. Beware steps—two steps. She stops. "Again," says Gran.

After seven steps like this Beware won't go any farther. Her back legs wobble. "Let's let her rest," says Lily. If Beware falls down, how could they ever get her up?

Gran asks, "Are we doing her any harm?"

"She doesn't seem any worse," Lily says. They stand in the growing darkness.

"All right, let's try again," Gran says after a minute.

Ten steps this time. For three of the steps Beware really walks, without their pulling or pushing.

She stops. "That looked better," Gran says. "Come on, girl, let's go!"

Stop and start, push and pull, they go down the hill. By the time they reach the bottom Beware is walking better. She still goes slowly, and she looks unhappy, but her back legs work much better now. What can be wrong with her? Lily has never heard of a sickness like this.

She opens the gate and leads Beware into the barn. Gran snaps the switch, and the cozy yellow light comes on. The light makes the barn look warm, but it isn't really.

CHAPTER THREE

Lily puts Beware in the crossties. Beware hangs her head until the two ropes are holding her up. Down here in the light Lily can see how sick she looks. Her eyes are dull, her ears droop, and she stands very still. What can be wrong? The only sicknesses Lily can think of are the worst ones. Sleeping sickness. Lockjaw.

Lily's teeth are chattering now, and she can't stop them.

Gran's hand squeezes Lily's shoulder. "Run inside and put a warm coat on."

Lily's legs feel heavy. It is a long climb up the path

to the house, and then the kitchen is so warm Lily wants to stay. There is apple crisp smell, and pot roast smell, and heat pouring off the iron sides of the woodstove.

She takes her barn jacket off its peg in the cellarway. The jacket feels tight when she puts it on. The last time Lily wore it was early last spring. She must have been smaller then. She finds her winter hat in the pocket, pulls it on, and goes outside.

Headlights are coming up the driveway—tall headlights. Lily waits. A white truck stops beside her. A short man with a beard steps down from the cab. "Hello, are you Lily? Tom Shore." He takes out his black doctor's bag and a small metal pail. "Can you fill this with warm water for me, Lily?"

Lily fills the pail at the kitchen sink. Then she leads Dr. Shore to the barn. "We got her inside. I hope it was okay to move her."

Gran waits next to Beware, looking out the open barn door. In Gramp's coat and his tall black boots

Gran doesn't look like someone who doesn't like horses. She looks like someone who knows just what to do.

"Hello, Tom," she says.

"Hi, Grace," says Dr. Shore. He sounds surprised. "Woody not home?"

"Not yet," says Gran. "You'll have to make do with Lily and me."

Dr. Shore opens his black bag. He takes out a thermometer and a stethoscope.

"She can't move her back legs—" Lily starts to explain.

"Don't tell me yet," Dr. Shore says. "Let me see what I can find."

Dr. Shore takes Beware's temperature. "Not too bad," he says. He looks at her teeth and gums. What can he be looking for there? Beware's teeth don't have anything to do with the way she was walking!

Dr. Shore puts the prongs of the stethoscope in his ears. He puts the flat, listening part on Beware's side, right where the girth of a saddle would go.

When the doctor did that to Lily, she got goose bumps. At least the metal isn't cold to Beware, with her fluffy winter coat on.

Dr. Shore moves the stethoscope back along Beware's side, up, down. He listens as he snaps his finger against Beware's side. Then he takes the prongs out of his ears and moves to the other side.

"Maybe it's her back," Lily says. If your back is broken, you can't move.

Dr. Shore shakes his head. He doesn't say anything, just moves along Beware's side: listening, thumping, listening.

Finally Dr. Shore straightens. "Well," he says, "looks like your mare's got colic."

Colic is a stomach ache, Lily knows that. It can be very dangerous. Horses can die of colic.

But it doesn't make sense. "It was her back *legs*," Lily says. "She couldn't move them! She wouldn't move at all!"

"She's bracing against the pain, Lily. Do you have any idea how long she's been sick?"

"She was all right yesterday," says Lily. Yesterday was Sunday, and she rode in the afternoon. This morning she put out hay for Beware and the pony, but they didn't come because they had grass to eat.

"So it could have been all day?" Dr. Shore holds a bottle up to the light and fills a syringe from it. "See, she's got a lot of gas trapped in the intestine, and it hurts. She was probably afraid to move."

"But look at this!" Lily points to the line of muscle along Beware's side. "Her belly doesn't look like this most of the time!" Beware's belly is round and fuzzy with her long winter hair, and she likes to be scratched. "And she isn't rolling or kicking at herself. I thought that's what horses with colic did!" Then Lily has to stop talking because if she doesn't, she is going to cry.

"Normally that is how horses react to colic," says Dr. Shore. "They kick at the belly because it hurts— just the way they might kick away a fly. If this weren't such a tough little mare, I think she'd be rolling and kicking, too. What she's doing is just bracing her whole body, holding herself super-still and stiff, hoping it'll go away. And it's going to, 'cause I'm going to give her a shot of painkiller right now." He pinches up a roll of skin on Beware's neck and slides the needle in. Beware's ears don't even twitch.

"Now I'm going to give her something to make her sleepy"—he gives Beware another shot—"and then we'll get something inside her to make whatever's blocking the intestine move along." He bends over the pail of water, squirts mineral oil into it, and mixes.

Lily hears Gramp's truck rattle up the driveway. It sounds as if lots of pieces are about to fall off. The engine turns off, and very quickly Gramp's footsteps come down the path.

He comes through the big barn door with his empty pipe upside down in his mouth. His old green hat is squashed down over his eyes. That's how he wears it when he's trading horses and doesn't want anyone to know what he is thinking.

"Oh, heck!" he says. "It's Beware."

Gran is standing against the stall door with her arms crossed. She and Gramp look at each other for a minute. Then Gramp comes to Beware's head and puts one arm around Lily.

"What's the trouble?"

"Oh, hi, Woody. Mare's got colic, lot of trapped gas—you're just in time to help me tube her." Dr. Shore takes a long plastic tube out of his bag, and next, a shiny steel bicycle pump.

Beware's head droops lower and lower. Her eyes are closing. One back leg shifts, and she almost loses her balance. Then the other leg shifts.

"She's getting dreamy," says Dr. Shore. "Couple more minutes."

"How long has she been like this?" Gramp asks.

"I found her after school," Lily says. "She wouldn't walk. Her back legs didn't work." She still feels the way she did alone with Beware on the hill. There is danger; she doesn't understand.

Dr. Shore says, "Now, Woody, you want to hold her head up?"

Lily stands beside Gran and watches Gramp lift Beware's head. He rests her jaw on his shoulder. Dr. Shore slips one end of the long plastic tube into Beware's nose.

Beware's eyes roll. She swallows, and swallows again, as Dr. Shore slides the tube down her throat. Lily reaches for Gran's hand.

"I had a nose tube that time I was in the hospital," Gran says. "Wasn't all that bad. Course, it was smaller."

Dr. Shore puts the other end of the tube into the bucket. He starts pumping with the shiny bicycle pump. The water goes up the tube and down Beware's throat to her stomach. "This is going to make whatever's blocking her shift along," Dr. Shore explains.

When the water is all gone, he gently slides the tube out. "You can let her go, Woody." Gramp lowers Beware's head until the crossties are supporting her.

"Now I want you to put a blanket on her," Dr. Shore says to Gramp, "and put her in a stall. She should be more alert in about half an hour. Give her some water, and keep an eye on her to see if she passes manure."

"How did you know it was colic?" Gramp asks. "I wouldn't have said that was what it was." That makes Lily feel better.

"Listen," Dr. Shore says. He points to a spot on Beware's side. "If you tap your finger right there, you'll hear a pinging sound, like a full propane tank. That's the sound of trapped gas."

Gramp taps and listens. Gran puts her hand on Lily's back and gives her a little push forward. "You should know, too," she says.

When Lily puts her ear against Beware's warm side, she doesn't hear anything at first. Then, as if far away, she hears some high, whiny pinging sounds inside Beware.

"Now, if you listen over here"—Dr. Shore goes to Beware's left side—"you won't hear anything. That's bad, too. You should be hearing some nice gurgly, rumbling sounds. She's blocked on the right side, and that's not letting anything through to the rest of the bowel. But that should start to change pretty soon now."

"Should I walk her?" Lily asks. That is what she's always heard you are supposed to do for a horse with colic—keep it walking.

"No, I don't think that's necessary," Dr. Shore says. "You do that to keep them from rolling, and this mare's not rolling. Just keep her warm and let her rest." He closes his bag with a snap. "And call the clinic if she doesn't pass some manure by morning."

"How soon should she start to get better?" Gramp asks.

"Soon," Dr. Shore says. "She's going to be better soon, or she's going to be a whole lot worse."

CHAPTER FOUR

W HEN HE IS GONE, Gran and Lily and Gramp just
stand for a moment looking at Beware. Beware's head
hangs low. Slowly, slowly she tips toward one side.
Then she catches herself and slowly, slowly tips the
other way. Her lips droop. Her ears flop limply.

"Well, let's get her comfortable," Gramp says.

Gran starts toward the door. "I'll get supper going.
You two come up when you're ready."

The blanket Gramp finds for Beware is big enough
for a workhorse. It reaches almost to the floor. A
mouse has chewed the edge, and the lining hangs
out.

Gramp helps Lily fold the blanket so it fits. Then he goes to get some baling twine. Lily lifts the blanket and listens to Beware's right side.

"You won't hear any change yet," Gramp says. "It'll take awhile." He ties the baling twine around Beware's middle. "There. Not handsome, but it'll stay." Gramp and Lily make a deep bed of shavings in the nearest stall, and they help Beware inside. "Let's go up and get some supper," Gramp says.

"You don't think she'll start to roll?"

"All she wants right now is not to fall down," Gramp says. "While that shot's working, she'll brace against it. She'll be all right."

The kitchen is warm, and it smells good. Lily is glad to sit down in a chair. Gran hands her a big plate with pot roast and red cabbage and potato, and Lily eats it all.

"Your mother'll be home around eight," Gran tells Lily. "She's working late at the store." While they eat, Gran tells Gramp about bringing Beware down the hill. "We weren't sure it was the right thing to do, Linwood," she says, "but it didn't seem to be doing her any harm."

Gramp smiles at her. "We'll make a horsewoman out of you yet, Gracie!"

"It would be strange if I hadn't picked up a thing or two living with you all these years!" Lily feels them both looking at her.

"Apple crisp?" Gran asks.

"Maybe I should go check her."

"Eat your dessert, Lily," says Gramp. "We haven't been up here but twenty minutes."

When Lily goes back to the barn, she is warmed up and full. Gramp walks down, too. Loose change jingles in his pocket. "She'll prob'ly be feeling better," he says. "We'll find a nice pile of manure in the corner, and she'll be asking for her hay."

But there is no manure, and Beware just stands there. She turns her face away when Gramp brings her the water pail.

"It'll take a little time," Gramp says. "Come on back to the house."

"I'll watch her," Lily says.

Lily sits in the corner of Beware's stall. The two walls push against her shoulders. The shavings smell fresh and piney. The barn is very quiet. Beware does not stir.

After a while Mom's car drives up, and Mom goes into the house. A few minutes later she comes to the stall door. "How is she?"

"The same, I think." Lily listens to Beware's stomach. It sounds the way it did before. The ridges of muscle are still tight along Beware's sides.

"Well, she's no worse anyway," Mom says. "I brought you some tea."

Lily wraps her cold fingers around the mug. The tea is milky and sweet. "I wonder if Beware would like some." In the summer Beware shared Lily's soda. Lily would pour a little in her hand, and Beware would lick it off. Lily pours a warm pool of tea into her palm and holds it out to Beware.

Beware's ears prick up. She sniffs the tea. Slowly she licks it off Lily's hand. Then she looks down at the hay on the floor in front of her. She winds a few strands into her mouth and chews.

"That's encouraging!" Mom says. "Come up and get warm, Lily. You can check her again in an hour."

In an hour the pile of hay is no smaller. There is no manure in the stall. Beware's belly is making exactly the same noises. She is no worse, but she isn't any better either.

"Well, I've seen sicker horses," Gramp says. "Why don't you go to bed, Lily? I'll check her again before I turn in."

Lily thinks maybe she should stay up all night. But what would she do? That is the worst thing about this. There is nothing she can do for Beware, nothing at all. She can't rub her, she can't walk her, and she can't even feed her.

Gramp thumps Lily on the shoulder. "Don't worry. She'll be better in the morning."

CHAPTER FIVE

Wʜᴇɴ Lɪʟʏ ᴡᴀᴋᴇs ᴜᴘ, it is early, and the house is quiet. Lily dresses quickly and runs downstairs. Big wet green tracks lead across the frosty lawn to the barn. Gramp is there already.

He is looking into Beware's stall. When he hears Lily, he turns and shakes his head. For a second fear reaches inside and squeezes Lily's heart.

"She seems about the same."

"Then she isn't worse?" Lily opens the stall door. Beware's ears twitch forward for a moment and then drop back. The pile of hay is still in front of her. The water pail is full. There are no tracks in the bright orange shavings and no manure. "She's no better," Gramp says, "and she ought to be."

Lily puts her ear against Beware's right side. The propane tank sound is still there. On the other side there is no sound at all. The two lines of muscle stand out. When Lily offers a handful of hay, Beware turns her face away, as if the sight of it makes her feel sick.

"Can I call the clinic this early?" Lily asks. "Will they be open yet?"

"There's somebody on call for emergencies," Gramp says.

Lily runs up the path. The cold air freezes her throat. Her mind feels frozen, too. With a cold red finger she dials the clinic number.

A strange voice answers. It's not the nice lady from last night. "This is the answering service. Give me your number, and Dr. Brand will call you right back."

Lily sits down to wait. Mom comes downstairs in her warm bathrobe. "No better?"

"She won't even try to eat hay," Lily says.

"Maybe a piece of carrot," Mom says. "She might—"

The phone rings loudly. Lily jumps and answers it.

"Hello, Dr. Brand here." Dr. Brand is the woman vet. Lily knows her. "Horse with colic?"

"Yes. She was sick last night, and Dr. Shore said she should be better soon, but she's just the same."

"Okay, tell me what he said it was, and what he did." Dr. Brand talks Lily through everything Dr. Shore did last night—listening to her sides, the shots, the nose tube.

"Have you been walking her?"

"He said not to," Lily says, "because she wasn't rolling. He said to let her rest."

Dr. Brand is quiet for a few seconds. Then she says, "I'd start walking her now if I were you. I'll be there in about an hour."

Lily hangs up the phone, and Mom hands her a bowl of hot cereal. "Eat this before you go out."

"We should have been walking her!" Lily says. "I

knew it!" She can't put even one spoonful of cereal in her mouth. It makes her feel just the way hay makes Beware feel.

Gramp is haying the other horses. "Dr. Brand says walk her!" Lily yells. She snaps a lead rope into Beware's halter and pulls. "Come on, Beware! *Walk!*"

"Whoa, Lily. Calm down." Gramp steps into the stall. "She's stood still all night. She'll be stiff, just like when you found her." Gramp puts his shoulder against Beware's rump. "All right, now."

Gramp and Lily push and pull Beware outside into the frosty morning. Beware hangs her head. She doesn't want to walk. "I'll get my whip," Lily says. Beware *has* to walk. Dr. Brand says so. But it seems horrible to haul her around and maybe even hit her when she is sick. When Lily has a stomach ache, she stays in bed, and Mom gives her ginger ale.

"I'll just push her along," Gramp says. "Lead her in a circle right here in front of the barn. Come on, little mare. It's the best thing for you."

Dr. Brand is a small woman with a thick black braid. The braid is streaked with silver, and Dr. Brand is getting wrinkles beside her eyes, just like Gramp. Those kinds of wrinkles come from working outside and squinting against the sun. They come from smiling.

"Hello, mare," she says to Beware even before she says hello to Gramp and Lily. She holds her hand out for Beware to sniff. Then she takes hold of Beware's halter, gently and firmly. She lifts Beware's lip and looks at her gums.

"If a horse is in shock, the gums change color," Dr. Brand explains. "Hers look pretty normal. That's a good sign."

Dr. Brand takes Beware's temperature. She finds Beware's pulse and counts, looking at her watch. "Vital signs aren't bad." She takes out her stethoscope and listens and taps all along Beware's sides, just the way Dr. Shore did.

"Well, we could tell a lot more if we could see

inside her," Dr. Brand says finally. "But I think Tom was right. She has an obstruction—a hard mass of food stuck over here on the right side of the bowel."

"Why would that happen?" Gramp asks.

"Sometimes they don't drink enough water. Sometimes in the fall they'll eat something strange along the edge of the pasture, when the grass is getting low—acorns, or some weed that forms a mass instead of moving through. Most times we don't know why, and it doesn't matter. We'll give her a shot for the pain and tube her again."

Dr. Brand doesn't give Beware a tranquilizer. Instead she gets out a twitch—a stick with a short loop of chain on the end. Gramp puts the chain around Beware's top lip and twists the chain tight. It squeezes and scrunches Beware's velvety lip. Beware's eyes show white around the rims. She stands perfectly still.

"It doesn't hurt, Lily," Dr. Brand says. "The pressure on the nerves makes her stand still. It's better than a shot because it wears off right away."

"Should have seen your gran when the doctors put *her* nose tube in!" Gramp says. "They put a twitch on her, too. Had to get the janitor in to hold it!"

Lily tries to smile because that is what Gramp wants. She holds the tube up while Dr. Brand pumps. In a minute all the water is inside Beware. Dr. Brand slides the nose tube out, and Gramp untwists the twitch. Beware shakes her head and steps away from him.

Dr. Brand says, "Give her water if she'll take any."

"Hay?" Gramp asks.

"I wouldn't like to put more food in on top of what's stuck," Dr. Brand says. "A wisp of hay, maybe, or a carrot—that might help get her system moving. And walk her."

"How much?" Lily asks.

"Half an hour, rest her a couple of hours, then walk her again. Gentle exercise can help the gut get moving."

"How come Tom Shore didn't tell us that?" Gramp asks. He sounds angry at Dr. Shore.

"Everybody has a different idea about colic," Dr.

Brand says as she packs her bag. "Some people think that it's cruel to make a sick horse walk and that it doesn't do much good. I think it helps, but none of us can see inside the body, so nobody's really sure." Dr. Brand looks at Lily. "Still, if she were my horse, I'd walk her."

"I will," Lily says.

"Call me if she doesn't pass some manure by late afternoon," Dr. Brand says. Then she laughs. "Funny, isn't it? I went to seven years of college so I could talk about horse manure. Oh, well. Everything is beautiful in its proper place."

As they start up toward the house, the school bus stops at the end of the driveway. Gramp just looks at Lily and shakes his head. The bus waits a moment with the door open. When Lily doesn't come, the door closes, and the bus rattles on down the hill.

CHAPTER SIX

Gʀᴀᴍᴘ ᴀɴᴅ Mᴏᴍ go to work, and the house gets very quiet. Gran washes dishes. Lily dries them. Then she puts on her coat again and goes down to the barn.

Beware stands where Lily left her. She isn't asleep, but she isn't wide awake either. She seems to be listening to something deep inside herself, and she hardly notices Lily.

"Beware," Lily says, "look." She holds up a bright orange carrot and breaks it in half. The broken carrot smells fresh and sweet. Lily holds out a piece for Beware.

Beware looks at the carrot. She takes a piece in her mouth and crunches, very slowly. Shreds of carrot drop into the shavings. Beware does not try to pick them up. When Lily offers her the rest of the carrot, she turns her head away.

"Oh, Beware," Lily says.

She folds back the blanket on Beware's right side and listens. She hears the whining, pinging sound. On the left side she hears nothing. It is like opening your eyes in the dark. Beware's stomach is pulled in tight. Her muscles make long ridges down her sides.

It will take more time, Lily tells herself. Dr. Brand is a good vet, but the medicine does take time. Time, and walking. Lily snaps a rope onto Beware's halter. "Come on, let's go!"

Lily doesn't have a watch. She leads Beware in a big circle in front of the barn, and she counts to herself. "One thousand one, one thousand two, one thousand three," all the way to sixty. In one minute she can go almost twice around the circle. So they have to make almost forty circles before Beware can rest.

Beware's step is heavy and slow. It gets even slower. Finally Lily has to go get her riding whip and show it to Beware. Beware isn't afraid of the whip, but when she sees it, she knows she must do what Lily says.

When Beware is back in the stall, Lily listens to her sides. They sound just the same.

Lily walks around behind the barn. The other horses are eating hay out of the big rack. Lily listens to the rustle as each horse gathers a mouthful of hay and the hard, grinding sound as they chew. She looks at the horse manure on the ground. Dr. Brand is right. In its place even horse manure is beautiful. If Lily could see some in Beware's stall, she would be very happy.

Gran thinks Lily should read a schoolbook since she is staying home today. Lily looks at her math for a while, but it doesn't make sense. The math she is doing today is clock math—a half hour walking, two hours of rest. It is walking math. Twenty slow circles in one direction, and twenty in the other.

When Lily goes back to the barn, there is no manure in Beware's stall. She hasn't drunk her water. The sounds inside her are just the same.

All day long Lily walks Beware, and rests her, and listens. The day gets grayer and colder, and the wind starts to blow. The circle in front of the barn gets dark and trampled. Lily's legs ache. She feels cold all the time, even when she's in beside the stove.

And Beware gets no better. Sometimes Lily can hear a tiny, faraway grumble in her left side, and sometimes she can't. But the pinging sound on her right side doesn't change. Whatever is blocking Beware's bowel doesn't move.

Lily is walking Beware again when the school bus goes by. When she gets back to the house, Gran says, "Mandy wants you to call."

"Lily!" Mandy says. "What's the matter?"

"Beware has colic." Now Lily starts to cry. Up to now she hasn't cried at all.

On the phone Mandy is quiet. Then she asks, "Lily . . . Lily, how sick is she?"

Lily can't answer. It doesn't seem possible that

Beware's life is in danger. She isn't rolling. She isn't groaning. In some ways she seems almost normal. But she might die. She really might.

"Oh, Lily," Mandy says, "I wish I could come over."

"She won't *eat* anything!" Lily says. She has almost stopped crying. "Not even a carrot."

"If I could come, I'd bring her cough drops," Mandy says. "Remember how she loved those herbal cough drops?"

Mandy sounds as if Beware is already dead. Lily sniffs and wipes her eyes. "I might still have some," she says. "Mandy, I have to go. I have to call the vet again."

Dr. Brand is at another farm, miles away. She has two more calls to make after that, and *then*, the lady at the clinic says, she will come see Beware.

Lily goes to the pantry, where Gran is mixing a cake. She finds the cough drop bag. There are four left.

"Dr. Brand coming again?" Gran asks. Lily nods.

"Your gramp has a lot of faith in her. If anybody can help your horse, she can."

But maybe no one *can* help Beware. For a minute Lily doesn't even want to go to the barn. On the way down she will start to hope. But when she opens the stall door, Beware will just be standing there, no better than before.

"Gran," Lily asks, "what was it like when you had your gallbladder? I mean, when you were sick, before they took it out?"

"I don't think it was much like a horse with colic," Gran says. But Lily doesn't know. From the outside it seems the same. Gran was hurting, and she seemed to look inside herself, not out at the world, just the way Beware is doing. And there was nothing Lily could do to help.

But when Gran was sick it was different, too. The ambulance came, and she was carried away to a hospital. Lily remembers a bed that adjusted up and down. She remembers the nose tube, and she remembers the IV—water with medicine in it that dripped down from a bag, through a tube and a needle into Gran's arm. Nurses kept coming into the room to look at Gran, to see if she was okay.

Beware has only the old barn, full of cobwebs, and a blanket that is too big for her. She has only a vet who is miles away and Lily.

"I'll come down with you," Gran says. She puts on Gramp's old coat and tall rubber boots, and they step out the front door together.

"Rain," Gran says, holding out her hand to catch some. Lily holds her hand out, too.

"Ice," she says.

They walk down to the barn together. How will she walk Beware now? Lily wonders. The old horse blanket isn't waterproof. It will get wet, and Beware will get cold.

Beware is just standing there, the way Lily knew she would be. She points her ears at them for a moment, and then her ears droop back again.

"She's no worse anyway," Gran says. But Beware should be better by now. Gran is just trying to make Lily feel better.

Lily takes a cough drop out of her pocket. She

holds it close, so Beware can see. She opens the tiny wrapper.

Beware points her ears again. "She remembers!" Lily says. "She remembers the wrapper sound!" Lily crinkles the wrapper as much as she can, and Beware's ears stay forward. Gently she nudges Lily's hand. Her soft upper lip pokes into Lily's palm and fumbles up the cough drop. Crunch! Crunch!

"Oh, Gran!" Lily says. She hunts in her pocket for another cough drop. Beware watches. Are her eyes a little brighter? Lily finds a cough drop. She crunches and crinkles the wrapper, and Beware nudges her hand, harder, this time. *Crunch! Crunch! Crunch!*

"I wouldn't give her any more," Gran says. "Wait and see what Dr. Brand thinks."

A cough drop is so small, Lily doesn't see how one more would hurt Beware. But maybe Gran is right. Beware nudges Lily's arm, and Lily says, "No more." And that is the first time things have been normal since this time yesterday.

CHAPTER SEVEN

THE RAIN COMES steadily. How can Lily keep Beware from getting soaked? In horse catalogs she has seen rain sheets for horses, but Gramp has only this old chewed blanket. If it gets wet, there is nothing else to put on Beware.

Lily explains to Gran, and Gran says, "Do you have to walk her?"

"Yes." Walking is the only thing Lily can do for Beware, and she will not let rain stop her.

"You could cut open a garbage bag and spread it over her, I suppose," Gran says. Then she looks at Beware and shakes her head. "No, you'd need two or three, and I don't know what's to keep them on."

Gramp has a blue tarp folded up in the barn. Lily looks at it, but it is much too big and very stiff and rattly. It would scare Beware to have the tarp put over her.

Lily tries to think. What else is big like a sheet, but not too big, and waterproof?

Oh!

No, Gran will never let her. Gran is not like Gramp and Mom and Lily. She doesn't love horses.

Lily turns around. Gran is leaning over the stall door. "I know, I know," she says, and she strokes Beware's forehead. Beware closes her eyes.

"Gran," Lily says. "Gran, can I take the shower curtain for her?"

Gran turns sharply. She has "No, of course not!" all over her face. But after a moment she says, "Oh, go ahead! I suppose I should be thankful it's not my best bed quilt you want!"

Lily and Gran splash up to the house. Gran helps Lily take down the shower curtain that goes all the way around the bathtub. The curtain was new this spring. It has big pink flowers on it. Gran looks at it for a moment. Then she pushes it into Lily's hands. "Take it! I'll call your mother at the store and have her bring home another bag of cough drops."

Lily is still walking Beware when Dr. Brand drives in. She follows her flashlight beam down the path, and she laughs when she sees the shower curtain.

But she doesn't laugh when she listens with her stethoscope. She looks much tireder than she did this morning, and she looks very serious. Gramp comes into the barn while she is listening. Gran is with him.

At last Dr. Brand takes the stethoscope out of her ears. She looks at them. "A horse this sick should be at Tufts," she says. Tufts is where the animal hospital is, where sick racehorses go. It's a long way away, and it's very expensive.

"Does she need surgery?" Gramp asks.

"I'm starting to think she does," Dr. Brand says. She shakes her head. "She needs something to happen soon, or she's just not going to make it."

Dr. Brand's words go through Lily's heart like a

spear. Not going to make it? Beware is *here*! She looks almost normal. Is she dying?

"How soon would we need to take her?" Gramp asks.

Dr. Brand squints at her watch. "We'll tube her one more time," she says, "but if you don't see manure by midnight, I'd load her in the truck and start. But, Woody, it'll cost you. You have to ask yourself how much the horse is worth to you."

Lily twists her fingers into Beware's long black mane. Gramp might say, "I don't care what it costs. Nothing's too good for Beware!" Lily knows he feels that way. But when you don't have money, you just don't. Your feelings don't change that.

"I'll get your warm water," Gramp says.

"How much would it cost?" Gran asks when he is gone.

Dr. Brand rubs her eyes. "Around a thousand if you don't do surgery. Probably three thousand if you do."

"That is a lot of money," Gran says.

"And surgery is risky," says Dr. Brand. "You might pay that money and not end up with a live horse."

Lily's face feels cold and stiff. Dr. Brand looks at her, and then she pats Beware's neck. "That sounds harsh, Lily. I'm sorry. But it's best to look squarely at these things."

Then Gramp comes in with the bucket, and Dr. Brand takes the twitch out of her bag. Beware shows the whites of her eyes and backs into the corner of the stall.

"Well! Still got some spunk!" Dr. Brand seems pleased.

When the tubing is finished and Dr. Brand has packed her things, she turns to Lily. "Keep walking her, and call me, okay? If she's not better by midnight, call me at home."

Lily can't speak. She can only nod. "Good luck," Dr. Brand says, and goes out into the dark. Gran and Gramp go with her.

Lily stands with her hands on Beware's neck. Beware's head is down, her eyes half closed. Lily thinks of the day Gramp brought her home. Lily knew right away that Beware would be hers, but Gramp was worried about her name. Why would anyone call a nice little mare Beware? Lily remembers the day she found out how Beware got her name; the day she rode with Mandy, and Beware tried to race the deer; the day of the horse show, when Beware jumped so beautifully and got a blue ribbon in the Flag Race. Is Beware's story going to end like this? Because of some stupid piece of food stuck inside her?

All at once Lily is angry, straight through. "Beware, you *stop* this!" she says. Beware's dull ears jump forward for a second. "You *get* better, Beware! You be well! You are *not* going to die, so you just *quit* this!"

Lily is yelling at Beware, in a whisper. Beware looks startled, and then she seems to get used to that sound in Lily's voice. Her ears droop again.

Someone is coming toward the stall. Lily expects Gramp, but it is Dr. Brand who opens the door. Her shoulders and her long black braid are covered with shiny ice pellets. She is carrying a plastic bag filled with something that looks like water.

"I decided to try one more thing."

CHAPTER EIGHT

THE PLASTIC BAG is like the IV Gran had in the hospital. It holds a saline solution, salt and minerals in water. "Since she won't drink, we'll just get this fluid inside her," Dr. Brand says. "That might perk her up and get things moving in her gut."

It is dark inside Beware's stall. The light from the aisle slants in over the door, on Dr. Brand's wet shoulders. What made her come back? Lily wonders. What made her decide to try something else?

"Oh!" Lily remembers. "Can I give her cough drops? This kind." She finds a cough drop in her pocket and shows it to Dr. Brand.

"Does she like them?" Dr. Brand asks.

Beware's nose reaches between them, and Lily closes her fingers around the cough drop. "Beware, wait! I have to take the wrapper off!"

Dr. Brand laughs. "Well! Anything she takes *that* much interest in has to be good."

"Hurry up, Lily!" Gramp says over her shoulder.

Beware is poking Lily's hand. Her eyes look brighter than they have all day.

Dr. Brand hangs the plastic bag on a nail high in the wall of Beware's stall. Now she takes out a shaver and shaves a patch on Beware's neck. "Bring the twitch, Woody."

Beware snorts and backs up when she sees the twitch. But she must stand still while the fluid goes in, and that will take awhile. Gramp twists the twitch around Beware's lip and holds it.

Carefully Dr. Brand finds a big vein. With a quick motion she sticks in a needle. Nothing is attached to the back of the needle. Blood squeezes slowly out of it. Then Dr. Brand fits the tube from the plastic bag onto the needle. Slowly, slowly the clear fluid starts to flow into Beware's vein. It seems strange to see the plastic bag hanging from a nail in the barn, instead of in a hospital. It's scary, too. But at least they are doing everything they can.

In the quiet stall Beware's breath sounds loud. She stands still, the fluid bubbles down, and they all wait. Dr. Brand yawns.

"Hope we don't have to wake you up tonight," Gramp says.

"Me, too! You'll have a long night, though. You've got to keep walking her." Dr. Brand yawns again and flicks the flowered shower curtain with one finger. "Funny!"

Finally the plastic bag is empty. Dr. Brand takes the needle out of Beware's neck. "Okay, Woody, you can let go." Gramp releases the twitch, and Beware backs away. She won't come near Gramp or Dr. Brand even when Lily unwraps the last cough drop. But when Lily brings the cough drop to her, Beware crunches it.

"She looks tired," Dr. Brand says. They are all tired. Lily and Gramp help Dr. Brand pack her things and carry them up to the truck.

"If she comes through the night in good shape," Dr. Brand says, "if she passes manure and seems to feel better, call me in the morning." She climbs into the high cab of her truck. The windshield wipers slap back and forth. The headlights make two dim cones out into the night and sleet. Dr. Brand drives away.

Gramp squeezes Lily's shoulder. "She's a good one," he says.

CHAPTER NINE

SUPPER IS MEAT LOAF, and Lily eats as much as she can. She has two helpings of potato, and she eats dessert, even though she doesn't have room. If she is going to walk Beware all night, she has to be strong.

Mom comes home just as Lily finishes. "Roads are slippery," she says. That's not good if they have to take Beware to Tufts.

Mom has two bags of cough drops for Beware and new flashlight batteries.

Lily looks at the clock. Half an hour before she must walk Beware again. She runs a hot bath and soaks until she is warm and pink all over. It is strange to be in the tub with no curtain around it.

Lily dresses carefully. She puts on tights and pants, a turtleneck and a sweater, so she will be warm. When she puts on her barn jacket, it barely fits over the sweater. Gran finds her an old jacket of Gramp's. Over that Lily puts on a rain poncho.

Now she is ready for her long night.

Beware stands just like before. Is there a little less water in her bucket? Lily can't tell. Maybe there is a tiny, far-off growl in the left side of Beware's stomach. Or maybe Lily is imagining it.

"Come on," Lily says. Her legs ache, and Beware's must, too. It is cold out, with wet snow falling. The snow melts when it touches the ground.

Beware plods with her head down. Around and around and around . . . Lily loses count and tries to guess how many circles. Ten? She stops and lifts the blanket to listen to Beware's right side. Sleet patters on the shower curtain. Lily puts her hand over her other ear. She doesn't hear the ping at first. Then it is there. But is it as loud as before?

"Come on, Beware. Got to keep walking."

A tiny flashlight beam comes slowly downhill from the house. Mom. She walks around the circle with Lily and Beware. They all keep their heads down. Lily and Mom don't talk.

"That's enough," Lily says finally. She leads Beware inside and listens to her stomach. Now she can't tell if there is any change. Beware turns her head away from the water pail. But when Lily reaches into her pocket for a cough drop, Beware pricks up her ears.

The next time Lily walks Beware, Gramp goes with her. They don't talk either. There is nothing to say after they have listened to Beware's belly. "A little better?" Lily wonders, and Gramp isn't sure.

Then Lily goes to bed. Gran wants Mom or Gramp to get up with her every two hours. But Lily says no. "I can do it."

She sets her alarm clock carefully. Ten o'clock is when she will get up, but Lily has never gotten up on purpose after she's gone to bed. Will the alarm go off? What if she sleeps through it? She lies under the covers, wide-awake, listening to the second hand tick. Sleet rattles against the house, and downstairs Gran, Gramp, and Mom are talking. About Beware? If Beware isn't better by midnight, what will they decide?

Gramp and Mom love Beware. Gran loves Lily. They will want to help. But do they have enough money?

And is it even the best thing for Beware, to put her in the truck for a dark, icy drive? Sometimes it is kindest to give up, Lily knows. That is what happened when their old dog Rip was hit by a car. Gramp and Lily drove him to the clinic as fast as the truck would go. Dr. Brand looked at him, and she just shook her head and got out her needle. Quietly Rip stopped panting, and they took him home and buried him. Gramp cried, Lily remembers. Gran didn't. But the next night she held her piecrust down, and no dog came to take it, and *then* she cried.

Lily could cry now. But crying would make her

feel helpless, and she has to be tough. She has work to do. She looks at the clock. Ten past nine. Lily closes her eyes and makes herself lie still.

Ngaaaah! goes the alarm. Lily jumps up. She feels wide-awake in an instant. She dresses quickly and follows the flashlight beam down to the barn.

Beware stands in her stall, the way she's been standing all along. She nudges Lily's pocket, and her eyes grow bright and soft while Lily unwraps a cough drop. But her stomach sounds no better. Lily presses her lips tight together. "Come on, Beware." They duck their heads and trudge out into the sleet.

After twenty circles Lily's hips ache. Her legs ache. Beware walks more and more slowly. Is this cruel? Lily wonders. Should she give up and just let Beware rest?

Lily lifts the blanket and puts her ear against Beware's warm side. Sleet rattles on the shower curtain, but within Beware it is quiet—

No, it isn't! A big, deep growl sounds beneath Lily's ear, like faraway thunder. Lily keeps her ear pressed to Beware's side. A minute later she hears another rumble.

"*Beware!* Oh, good girl!" Smiling makes Lily's cold cheeks ache. Sleet rattles on her front teeth. She listens to Beware's right side, too. The pinging sound is not so bad. The walking is starting to work.

"Come on, Beware!" Lily says. "Twenty more circles to go!"

CHAPTER TEN

"How's she doing?" Gramp calls from the bedroom when Lily comes back in.

"Her stomach is growling!"

"That's good," Gramp says. "When you go out at midnight, wake me up." He says something to Gran, and after a minute Gran answers. They still have not decided what they will do at midnight if Beware is not better. Lily can tell by the sound of their voices, even though she can't hear a word.

* * *

Waking up at midnight is hard. The dark seems blacker than before, and the house is colder. A big wind blows the sleet loudly against the house.

Lily goes softly past Mom's room. "Dress warmly, Lily," Mom says. The light is already on in Gran and Gramp's room, and they are talking softly. "I'll be right down, Lily," says Gramp.

Lily puts more cough drops in her pocket and goes down the path to the barn. She snaps on the light, and then she stands with her hand on the switch. She doesn't want to go to the stall door. She doesn't want to see Beware standing there no better than before. She doesn't want to face the storm, and putting Beware in the truck, or deciding not to.

But there is no choice. Slowly Lily walks toward the stall.

Beware nickers loudly and leans out over the half door. She reaches toward Lily and tosses her head.

"Beware!" Lily pushes Beware back and steps inside the stall. The deep shavings look messed up, as if Beware has been moving around. Has she been rolling? Was she pacing in pain? Lily bends to look more closely.

Beware nudges her pocket. "Beware, quit it!" Tiredness is like a cold fog in Lily's head. What is going on? She isn't quite sure.

"Well, look at that!" Gramp is standing at the half door. His green hat is squashed onto the back of his head, and he has a great big tired smile on his face. "I never in my life thought I'd be so happy to see a pile of horse manure!"

Poke! Beware shoves at Lily's pocket.

"Give that mare a cough drop!" Gramp says. He's in the stall now. His arm goes around Lily. Tears spill hot on her cheeks.

Shove! Beware almost rips the pocket off Lily's coat.

"Hey!" Lily sniffs. "You're really picking up some bad habits, Beware!"

It is still important to walk Beware. Her stomach doesn't sound quite normal. But it is so much better that Gramp and Lily have to catch one of the other horses and listen to compare.

"Go to bed," Gramp says. "I'll do it."

"No, I want to," Lily says, and Gramp smiles.

"Course you do. You're doing a good job, kid! See you in the morning."

Forty circles in front of the barn are still long and cold. Lily's legs are still tired, and so are Beware's. The mud is slippery. The sleet is cold on Lily's face. The wind blows.

But Beware is going to be all right. When Lily puts her in the stall, she can hear Beware's stomach growl from six feet away. She gives Beware one more cough drop, and she kisses Beware on the end of her soft, whiskery, cough drop–smelling nose. "See you in two hours."

At two o'clock, and four-thirty, Lily gets up. The short stretches of sleep seem to make her more tired. Her eyes prickle. She feels cold, and even in bed with her clothes on, she doesn't get warm.

But Beware is getting better. She is tired and cross. She has eaten half a bag of cough drops, and every time Lily's hand moves she looks for another one. But she is better, and at four-thirty the sleet has stopped. The sky is getting gray when Lily climbs back up the hill, and when the smell of breakfast wakes her up, the sun is shining.

Gramp is just coming indoors when Lily gets down to the kitchen. His hat is on the side of his head, and Lily can tell before he speaks that Beware is all right.

Dr. Brand heaves a big, slow sigh when Lily tells her. "Oh, good. I didn't feel happy about you and Beware when I went to bed last night."

Lily still has to walk Beware, but not as often. She has to get bran and have Gramp show her how to make a bran mash. And they'll have to keep close watch on Beware for the next few days. She may have some bruising inside her, and the colic could come back. But Dr. Brand doesn't need to see her again. "Congratulations to both of you," she says.

"Thank *you*," Lily says. "You saved her life."

Dr. Brand laughs. "It's just as likely it was the cough drops! Stay in touch."

As soon as Lily hangs up the phone, it rings. Mandy is calling. "Beware is going to be okay," Lily says. "The cough drops helped." And she tells Mandy all about it.

"Are you coming to school?" Mandy asks.

"No," Lily says. Today she will stay home and walk Beware. If she went to school, she would only fall asleep.

"Then I'll get off the bus at your house tonight," Mandy says. "I'll bring Beware an apple."

"Going to see your horse?" Gran asks when Lily hangs up the phone. Gran does not usually believe in horses before breakfast, but now she hands Lily a hot, buttered muffin. "Eat this on your way down."

Lily puts her coat on and goes outside. The big gray clouds are breaking up, and sun streaks in beneath them. The patches of snow on the ground make the grass look very green. A rain shower starts and stops in the time it takes Lily to walk to the barn.

Beware is looking over the stall door. She nickers

to Lily. Her eyes are bright. Her ears prick forward. She pushes against the stall door, and the shower curtain crackles.

"You're spoiled, Beware!" Lily says, and breaks off a piece of muffin for her.

Now that Beware is better, Lily can see how sick she really was. It's scary. Lily feels as if she is bruised inside, too. Beware didn't die, but she could have. She came close. The sun shines, the rain comes down, and Lily knows that, after this, nothing will ever seem quite the same.